MARVA VARMA.

TIME AND FATE.

RITHIK VISHVARAJ M H

Contents

Genre, Logline, And Synopsis

STORY PLOTS:

INVESTIGATIVE THRILLER, DARK COMEDIES, SCI-FI(TIMELOOP AND DEJAVU).

LOGLINE:

A fearless CRIMINAL LAWYER stuck in DEJA VU and the mind-blower criminal police officer stuck in a TIME LOOP. The criminal lawyer wants to make more SUPERSTITIONS in his life to survive his life and the criminal police officer wants to make some changes to the superstition practiced by the criminal lawyer to escape from a GREAT THREAT.

SYNOPSIS:

This is the story narrates when the time and the fate decide our life journey. there is a criminal police officer who finds more mysteries and leads to the right decision. his name is VINAY Marvan. there is another guy who is opposite and different from Marvan. he is a criminal lawyer, his name is RAMA Varman. Marvan is sincere in his detective job. he reports all the cases on time and closes the cases within a particular period. Varman is a rough, violent, and rigid(RVR) guy. Varman blames all his mistakes on someone and he doesn't respect others' words. he wishes for what he wants. Varman had a fiance, named Priya. she died in a road accident at midnight. Varman changed his behavior to very rugged. Varman wants to know how she died. Varman investigated the midnight scenario. and he finally thought that it couldn't be an accident rather it could be planned murder. Varman wants the help of police and detective agents but no one helped. so he thought to police wanted to pay attention to him. he planned to kill a MORTUARY DOCTOR named as DR.KALIDASSAN(8:20 AM). the police officers arrested

TWO BIKE THEFT GUYS(BASKAR(BOSS) AND MURUGA) for this case(because the theft happened exactly at the same time and near the location). Varman for a purpose surrendered to the police for this murder, and Marvan was placed to investigate Varman. Marvan investigated Varman by asking questions but no encouraging answer was engaged from Varman(10:10 AM). Varman asked for a chess game set up. if he loses the coins, he will give some clues to Marvan's case. Marvan doesn't know how to play chess. but know he wants to be more conscious to defeat Varman. and Marvan should say about the other cases and his personal life. the game begins.

Marvan starts the game by attacking a soldier. Varman plays a bold play in chess. Marvan defeated one soldier of Varman and Varman gives a clue "I am not a known person to you,(personally)". next Varman predicted the next move of Marvan and played a safe game and defeated a soldier of Marvan. Marvan went back to the time when he didn't start the investigation of Varman. he was frustrated and he learned every mistake that he did in the game. but the thing is Varman knows to predict the move by using his moments that happened in previous visuals or deja vu. for every time Marvan gets a phone call but he avoids it. Marvan commits mistakes and forgets the clues he gained from Varman, again he investigates and plays chess with him and commits mistakes. Marvan was so angry at Varman. like that he made plenty of mistakes and learned from them. he played more games in different time loops. Varman gave more clues to Marvan. Marvan finally made a checkmate in the game, but Varman said that checkmate is not for the end of the game. the real game finishes only the king is defeated. so Varman made a knight kill the king of Marvan, and he came to the same time loop. now he thought to deal carefully with the game. he thought that he play a half-game when the phone call rang, he can make changes in Varman's superstition and prediction(deja vu), he can guess what clues he said for this case and he can escape from the time loop.

Marvan's plan worked but the thing is Varman escaped from the police investigation room. Varman called Marvan via call and said that his next target is Abi Vighoran. Abi Vighoran is a criminal detective who solved more mysterious cases. Vighoran killed Priya portrayed as an accident. he killed Priya because she made money by kidnapping. this money kidnapping is a new concept which means some currency notes have fancy currency numbers. these numbers are not used as a currency lender. it acts as a business. because these numbers can hack the security privacy of our nation. these numbers are sold to higher-class people for a collection. even some currencies can have some secret security code for the government of India. so a terrorist came here for this purpose and asked for money from Priya, so the terrorist asked Vighoran to follow her. after she knows the money lender is a terrorist, she avoids giving the money so the terrorist asked Vighoran to kill Priya. and finally, Vighoran was assassinated by Varman. At that moment Marvan arrived there. they had a fun talk between them. then finally Varman says about his old fiance's case that holds up by Marvan. Marvan doesn't take the case seriously. he had his attention on only to finish the case. dr.Khalidhassan gave a wrong mortuary report on this case, so Marvan closed the file with a dead-end justification. for a correct justification Varman wants to play a brutal role against Marvan, so he collected the clues from Marvan and re-investigated the case for the right judgment for his fiance. he thought to investigate dr. Khalidhassan but before he goes he was killed. yes, he didn't kill Khalidhassan, so the next choice and the final choice of investigation is Marvan. to approach Marvan he surrenders for the murder of Khalidhassan. because of Varman's active investigation, Marvan killed Khalidhassan and also framed two bike thefts for this case, but in the middle Varman came into it. because of his name, he did it. he asked why Marvan did it for this case. the answer is only some cases come to the police that is only small petty cases. On behalf of other cases is scheduled be, detective agents, and criminal lawyers. these cases are not given to handle to the police because it spoils the name of the affector and criminal in the press and newspaper. and police have high pressure to finish the case, if not transfer it to CBI and criminal courts. so Varman knows that Marvan killed Khalidhassan. and Marvan knows that Varman killed Vighoran. so both pointed the target on both sides' heads. and finally, a gunshot sound is heard. the end.

CHAPTER ONE

SCREENPLAY

SCENE 1:INT|INVESTIGATION OF THE BIKE THEFTERS|(8:10 AM):

VINAY MARVAN entering to the police custody. there the police are saluting Marvan. the police are investigating the bike thefters - they are BASKAR(BOSS) AND MURUGAN.

POLICE

un peru enaya?

MURUGAN

Murugan sir. studied mechanic engineering for past 4 years sir, 4 arrears inum iruku sir, amma peru..(attention).

BASKAR

apidiye un adhar card um un ration cardiyum uh kuduthu viden adthu 2 varshathuku avangaluku achu use agum.

MURUGAN

en boss? ethachu namaku tour kupitu povangala boss.

BASKAR

Ama namaku tour kupitu poi vitu than aduthu velaye papanga, naane namala adthu 2 varshathuku entha jail ah veika porainga solli bithi la iruken ithula nee tour veraya unnaku.

POLICE

Un peru enna da?

MURUGAN

En boss eh mariyathai illama koopriya nee. pathathahuku avera kadupethriya nee.

BASKAR
dei naan eppa da kadupanen
MURUGAN
nee gumunu iru ivane
POLICE
mavane romba panninga, kannu mattum than irukum mathathelum urichiruvom. oru bike kooda thiruda therla ungaluku.. chi.. pera sollu
BASKAR
oru nimisham sir.. nee ennaye oru vaati kuda nee ena mathichathela un kallula kuda viluguren please konja neram amaithiya iru.
BASKAR
Basker sir..
MURUGAN
apadi enna thapa sonam?
mm..perula than boss ivaru verum dummy piece.
BASKAR
same to you da mechanic.
ellathiyum senjitu enna thapu senjom ah. ivana than vechikitu.. enga koondu vanthu niruthikiya pathiya nee.
Murugan and Baskar sat on the bench.
They imagine about their before arrest.
CUT TO FLASH BACK:
SCENE 2:EXT|BIKE THEFT|(7:30 AM):

Both Baskar and Murugan went to theft a bike in a roadside bike parking area. They was first failed it the next time a they opened the lock of the bike. When Baskar tried to sit on it, he dashed a vehicle nearby and alerted the whole area. Soon Murugan drived the bike without Baskar and slipped on nearby police jeep. Baskar act as a casual man but Murugan gave an indication to the police officers that Baskar is his boss

BASKAR
Dei takunu vandiya edra
MURUGAN

boss irunga naane steiring enga irukunu pakuren

BASKAR

Dei bike la enga da steiring uh. un naambi than da plan poten. nee oru mechanic than da sonne.

MURUGAN

boss naan mechanical engineering padichiven, mechanic illa (angry)

BASKAR

Seri takunu velaya paru da. ithuku onnum karachal illa.

MURUGAN

irunga boss innonu theditu iruken

BASKAR

Ippo enna?

MURUGAN

ANHH bike owner ku arive illa boss. Bike uh inga vechane athuku kuda bike saviyum vechirintha namala maari bike thefters ka easy yah irukumla.

BASKAR

Dei nee than 4 arrear vechirupiya doubt ah iruku da.

MURUGAN

En boss? naan all pass aiyurpen nenaichingala

BASKAR

Nee than 40 arrear vechirunthalam doubt eh illa da. vandiya seekrama edra

MURUGAN

Boss vandi start aiyurichu erunga

BASKAR

poda poda poda vandiye eduda

Baskar dashed a car and alerted by signaling all over the area. soon Murugan take the bike and left the Baskar and Murugan dashed a police jeep and

MURUGAN

AIYIYOOOO...

BASKAR

naan than sonnen vandiye edukka ana yaarukitta sonathalam thapa pochu. vendru paiya. poi savatum ivan than. aiyoo police uh ivana nambi first plan eh out.

MURUGAN

Sir avar than sir ennoda boss uh.

baskar

aiyayoo mattivitane seri apidiyea casual ah povom

POLICE OFFICER

Dai Baskar olunga inga vada illa adichu illuthuviduven jeep la

BASKAR

Entha branch sir? odane kandupidichitinga paravalaye.

This is the flashback of them why they came for the police station.

CUT TO.

SCENE 3:INT|VINAY MARVAN'S ENTRY|(10:00 AM):

MURUGAN

Boss modhalali enga boss?

BASKAR

modhalali ya? police ku enga da modhalali. aiyoo!..

MURUGAN

Boss oru bike theft ke oru boss uh, oru assistant irukum pothu, ivlo periya department ithu appana modhalali irukunama illaya. pathathukku naan than neriya company ku vela pathukriken boss.

BASKAR

apadi sir enga vela paathinga.

MURUGAN

jewellery kadai boss.

BOSS

unnaye ethuku sethanga nu ennaku ippo than da purithu.intha nee kettiye modhalali anga vararu paaru.

VINAY MARVAN'S ENTRY

MARVAN

yaaru sir ivaynga pudhusa irukanaga

police

namakunu varainga sir kalaila kuda vida matringa ivingala namaku pathi vazhkai tholaiya ve iruku sir. bike theft case sir.

MARVAN

iruya ivingala mattum than atleast konjam achu nama vela oditu iruku ivingalam sethu oru naal seivom ya. enga sir bike theft nadanthuchu?

POLICE

sir k.k.nagar la.

MARVAN

k.k.nagar ah..

POLICE

ama sir.

MARVAN(STRECHES his ARMS AND LEGS)

seri naan poitu moonji ya kaluvitu varen, vanthu visarikiren ivingala rendu perum, romba tried iruku.

Marvan go to restroom and washes his face. Meanwhile baskar and murugan stared each other and blinking their eyes.

suddenly a news come to the police station. A mortuary doctor named kalidhassan has been killed by someone. the news was carried to Marvan, when he was is in restroom. soon another news was carried to the police station. the news is that the murderer was surrendered to the police station.

POLICE

sir sir sir sir..

MARVAN

ennaya?

POLICE

sir nama police mortuary reports kudukara doctor kalidhassan kondutanga

MARVAN

ennaya solra.

POLICE

ama sir.

MARVAN

iruya velila varen

POLICE

kollapanaven ipo than sir surrender aiyurkan.

MARVAN

ennathu kolapanaven surrender aiytan ah.

POLICE

ama sir.

MARVAN

ennaya soldra.

POLICE

ama sir vanthu avana visaringa sir.

MARVAN

varen ya varen ya.

Marvan washed his face twice after hearing this news and go to the investigation room.

There a guy sitting in very ruged manner. His name is RAMA VARMAN.

CUT TO.

scene 4:int|first investigation between marvan and varman|(10:10 AM):

Marvan went to the investigation room quickly and started his investigation.

MARVAN

hey nee yaaru? unkam kalidhassanukum enna samatham? en avna konna.

varman

SILENT.

MARVAN

ennaya unnum pesa mattingaran

POLICE OFFICER

sir vanthathulirunthu onnume pesa mattingaran. aven perum avan than kollapanna mattum than soldran thavra vera ethuvum sollamatingaran sir.

MARVAN

edhachu two wheeler illa four wheeler vehicle oda vanthana.

POLICE OFFICER

ama sir two wheeler oda vanthan sir.

MARVAN

seri athula irukara no. plate ah verify pannunga.

POLICE OFFICER

okay sir.

MARVAN

ivanoda details pathi therinchittu vaanga quick.

POLICE

okay sir.

VARMAN

apidiye velila irukara atha bike theft pannavingalum koopudu.

MARVAN

yaaru nee ennaya order pannra.

VARMAN

SILENT.

MARVAN

avingala kooputu vaanga.

POLICE

seringa sir.

The police officer went out of the location and called the bike thefters to go inside the investigation room.

the police officers went to his table and searched the no. plate.

POLICE

dei rendu perum olla pongada sir koopudraru.

MURUGAN

ethuku naanga poganum athan innorutharu visarikarula

BASKAR

ithu un veedu illa police station please avinga pecha kelu.

naanga porom sir.

MURUGAN(m.v)

iven boss ah illa loosu ah evano sonna pecha kekuran paru.

BASKAR

ennaku kekuthu da idupattu paiyle.

MURUGAN

apo loosu than.

BASKAR

enda?...

MURUGAN

pinna mindvoice pesuren ennake kekathu unnaku mattum kekuma ah.

BASKAR

seri vanthu thola.

Baskar and Murugan entered to the investigation room.

BASKAR

sir neengala.

VARMAN

enada intha pakkom.

MARVAN

unnaku avingalakum ena samanthham. ivinga than nee ketta antha bike thefters, nee konna kalidhassan area la kalaila panniriukanga.

VARMAN

avingala inga ukara sollu.

MARVAN

dei neenga anga ukarunga da.

MURUGAN

keelaiye naangala en boss evlo periya aalu avara poi keela ukara solligitu. enga rendu chair podunga.

MARVAN

en un boss ku kaal illaya.

Marvan slaps baskar.

BASKAR

pothuma ippo unnaku santhosham thane. please thaivu senju ukaru illa vaila asinga asingam ah vanthurum.

Baskar and Murugan sat on the floor. Baskar sat oppositely to Marvan in one tile. Murugan sat oppositely to Varman in another tile. ONE TILE DIFFERENTIATION. LOCATION WISE TIME LOOP OCCURS.

After few seconds, the police enered the room with details of Varman.

POLICE

sir ivenoda details ellam kedaichirichu sir.

MARVAN

mmmmm... procede.

POLICE

sir iven peru Rama Varman sir. Madurai than sir ivenoda sontha ooru. iven oru criminal lawyer sir. neriya cases iven vathadiye solve aiyuruku sir.

MARVAN

criminal lawyer ah..

POLICE

ama sir ippo recent ah ivenoda activites ethaliyum check panna bodhu active vaveh illa. iven avenoda cases kooda koraichitan sir.

MARVAN

korachittan ah engayo idikithe. seri ivana naan pathukiren.

POLICE

okay sir.

MARVAN

apo nee oru criminal lawyer. en peru marvan, Vinay Marvan unnaya maari naanum oru criminal police officer assistant commisioner. seri vishayathuku varen nee en kalidhassan ah koona.

VARMAN

un mind la ekachakum manna kelvi kal vanthurikum athuku than ennala ovvanukum pathil solla mudiyathu. venum na oru chess game velayaduvom athula naan ovvaoru coinum lose panna lose panna naan unnaku hints tharen intha case la.

MARVAN

what? are you kidding? oru murder pannitu chess game velayadunum soldra.

VARMAN

if you want to know about me, then play a chess game with me....

MARVAN

(deep breath)

sir namma kitta irukara antha chess board eduthutu vanga.
the police immediately took the chess board and coins and come back to the investigation room.

POLICE

sir inthanga sir.

MARVAN

intha nee kettiye chess board athu inga iruku.

VARMAN

okay un coins ah nee arrange pannu.

MARVAN

ennaku chess velayada theriyathu.

varman

paravala naan arrange panra maari neeyum arrange pannu.
Varman choosed black and marvan choosed white.
Varman and Marvan were arranging the the coins.
meanwhile, Baskar and Murugan

MURUGAN

boss mess uh kelvi patruken athu enna chess uh.

BASKAR

nee oru madurai kaaran solli nirubidichita..

MURUGAN

eppadi boss.

BASKAR

pinna mess na madurai thanda ithu chess uh da.

POLICE

shhhhhhh......

MARVAN

ellam arrange panniten

VARMAN

ennaku ellam okay ana ennaku queen eh illa.

MARVAN

sir enga sir antha coin uh?

POLICE

illa sir athu romba nalla kanom sir.

VARMAN

okay paravala naan en ring ah use pannikiren queen ku pathila.

LET THE GAME BEGINS...

MARVAN

naan start pannava

VARMAN

mmm.. go ahead.

Marvan moves his first coin(solider) towards Varman.

Varman moves his first coin(solider) towards Marvan.

Marvan moves his second coin(solider)towards varman.

Varman moves his second coin(solider) towards Marvan.

Marvan moves his third coin(solider)towards varman.

Varman moves his first coin(solider) forward.

Marvan defeats a coin from varman.

VARMAN

chess velayada theriyathu sonna, a nice play. okay.

VARMAN

oruthananoda kannu kanam na avanuku kannu therla na kooda paravala ana vazhkaye sandikira nimisham therla na aven vazhra vazhkai latchiyum illatha vazhkai. NOW IT IS MY TURN.

Varman uses his superstition and predicts to defeat a coin from marvan(not here).

Varman defeats a coin from Marvan.

Suddenly Marvan switched to the bathroom and the time was 10:10 AM. this is the first time when the investigation not yet started. Not only marvan with him baskar also was switched where he sat. This is the first timeloop happened for both.

CUT TO.

SCENE 5:SECOND INVESTIGATION BETWEEN MARVAN AND VARMAN

POLICE

sir sir sir sir..

MARVAN

kalidhassan ah kondutangla

POLICE

ama sir.

MARVAN
ennaya soldra?
POLICE
ama sir.
MARVAN
iruya velila varen
POLICE
kollapanaven ipo than sir surrender aiyurkan.
MARVAN
thirumbayum varman surrender aiytan ah.
POLICE
ama sir.
MARVAN
ennaya soldra.
POLICE
ama sir vanthu avana visaringa sir.
MARVAN
varen ya varen ya.
Marvan washed his face twice after hearing this news and go to the investigation room.
Again RAMA VARMAN sitting in very ruged manner.
meanwhile baskar and murugan,
BASKAR (frustated)
ahhhan.. nama enga irukom.
MURUGAN
yo ennamo 10 varusham coma la iruntha maari panra.
BASKAR
dei nama antha room la thanda irunthom.
MURUGAN
arivu iruka unnaku namale police station le irukom unnaku room vera kekutha...
BASKAR
dei loosu maari pesathada ivlo neram antha A.C room le thanda irunthom.
MURUGAN

(he sees the fan rotating in the hall, it rotates slowly.)
oru hotel ku ponna A.C kekalam thappu illa ana fan ke inga valillama namala maari bike thefters ku ithulam theviya.

BASKAR

loosu payanayum lucha payanayum koodave vechathu evlo periya thappuntu ennaku ipa thanda purithu.

MURUGAN

boss naan sonnathu correct thane.

BASKAR

mmmmm.....(roar).

CUT TO.

ENTER TO THE INVESTIGATION ROOM.

POLICE OFFICER

sir vanthathulirunthu....

MARVAN

onnume pesa mattingaran. aven perum avan than kollapanna mattum than soldran thavra vera ethuvum sollamatingaran athane sir.

POLICE OFFICER

ama sir...

MARVAN

ennaku ivana pathi theriyum.

varman saw marvan doubtfully.

MARVAN

iven peru Rama varman, sontha ooru Madurai, iven oru criminal lawyer . neriya cases iven vathadiye solve aiyuruku.

VARMAN

parvalaiye ennaye pathi neriya therinthu vechikira pola.

MARVAN

unnaku antha bike theft um oru chess board thane venum. sir antha bike thefters rendu perum athukaprm antha chess board um konduvanga, quick.

VARMAN

parvalaye naan adthu enna sola poren therinthu vechikira. unnaku intha maari deja vu illa prediction illa superstition antha maari ethachu power iruka enna?

MARVAN

antha maari power iruntha naan than eppoyo saamiyar aiyuripen nithyanandha maari.

VARMAN

correct aiyurpilla..

MARVAN

game ethachu kaatriya.

VARMAN

game kaatala vilaydalam va.

the bike thefters and the chess board again come back.

MURUGAN

boss parunga visarika apove A.C podranga boss. apana namma rendu perum thenam thenam oru petti case la mattvum apa than daily A.C poduvanga boss, jolly yah irukom boss.

BASKAR

dei arrear gammunu vada sir vera ethachu thitti vida poraru.

MARVAN

dei rendu perum anga..

BASKAR

utkarunom athane sir.

MURUGAN

nee en apove A.C room keten purinchirchu boss.

BASKAR

iruda mavane kundila bomb veikiren.

MARVAN

sir neenga konjam velila irunga iven ah naan pathukiren.

POLICE

okay sir.

MARVAN

neenga coins ah arrange pannuga. athula queen illa unga ring ah use pannikonga queen pathila.

VARMAN

mmmmm.... un move than

MARVAN

okay let me start.

Marvan defeats a coin from varman.

VARMAN

naan clue sollanum la.

MARVAN

ama..

MURUGAN

boss glue kelvi patruken athu enna clue.

BASKAR

clue na hint uh da

MURUGAN

ohh athuku innoru peru vera iruka

BASKAR

ethuku?

MURUGAN

mint boss, mint mint mint uh... athan puthina.

BASKAR

ada eruma mattu paiyale naan achu nalavuthu than padichen intha naai naalu varsham engineering padichiven vera soldran athuvum MECHANICAL ENGINEERING vera. athulayum naalu arrear vera.

MURUGAN

ena boss?

BASKAR

illa nee kai kari kadaila velapakorpe nee nalla padichipan tu nenaichen.

VARMAN

athey kannu theriyathaven, avenoda kekum sakthi elanthana avenoda lachiyum illatha vazhkai irundupoi arthame illama poyirum. ippo en chance.

Varman uses his superstition and predicts to defeat a coin from marvan.

Varman defeats a coin from Marvan.

Again Marvan switched to the bathroom.

Baskar switched to the bench.

CUT TO.

SCENE:6:INT|THIRD INVESTIGATION BETWEEN MARVAN AND VARMAN|(10:10 AM):

Marvan was totally confused. why did he repeating the same time period.

Later he analysis that he looped only if he loses a coin in chess against varman.

Marvan took a glance and finds that if he loses a coin in past time loop, and if the same coin loses again he does not looped another time.

So at last if he want to escape from this great threat(time loop, he want to defeat varman's superstion or varman's chess play.

POLICE

sir..

MARVAN

enna kannadhassan eh kondutangla.

POLICE

ama sir.

MARVAN

kondaven station la surrender aiytana.

POLICE

ama sir.

MARVAN

naan soldra maari pannunga aven irukara room la oru chess board veinga.

Baskar also was confused. he look on to Murugan.

Murugan turned back and took a pen and write his name on the wall.

baskar

dei ennada panra?

murugan

boss en peru eludiren boss.

baskar

un peru ah? ethuku da?

murugan

ennga amma enga ponalum muthiram pathika solluvanga.

baskar

unga appa ena moothirum poga sonnanga la.

murugan

boss, en peru murugan, naalu varsham...

baskar

pothum da pothum.. pathi pathi naan onnum disturb panala.

baskar(m.v)

naane nadantha sambavum thirumba thirumba nadanthuttu iruku ithula iven vera. velila vada mavane kundi kula bomb veikiren.

murugan

boss apidiyea unga perum eluthi vidava jolly ah irukom.

baskar

en peru uh than eluthi ena medal ah ada vanga pora. nee eludhu eldhu un peru mattum eludhu.

baskar

dei naan keta thapa nenaika mattela

murugan

kelunga boss.

baskar

nama ena school illa college ku ka vanthirikom. nama vanthathu police station da.

murugan

athuku uh?...

baskar

en intha vetti polapu gummunu iruklamla. theveillama panni en ipadi time waste panra.

murugan

boss aduthu vaati varapo juniors ah rag panni nama than senior intu gethu ah solliklamla.

baskar

ama nama seniors, varavinga juniors, inga vela pakuravunga ena professors ah. dai ithu police station da!.. varavinga than professional murderers avinga kitta than un velaiye kamicha police station kooda paakama vaguthalaye koothuvanga.

MURUGAN

etha?..

BASKAR

kaathiye sonnen da panni.

MURUGAN

boss, nee romba dummy piece ah iruka, ipadi than en college la pannom.

BASKAR

eppo? narpathu varshathuku munnadi ya.

MURUGAN

boss, naan naalu varsham mechanical engineering padichiven, naalu arrear inum iruku.

BASKAR

sopa un pooranatha nipatu da.

MURUGAN

unhhh...(ugh)

BASKAR

ena unhh..

suddenly a radio was tuninng on. there the radio jockey was telling a information(related to the timeloop.).

baskar is going to tune off the radio.

MURUGAN

boss.....(screaming).

BASKAR

ena da? ippadi kathira

MURUGAN

illa boss thiderenu antha radio on acha athan kaathiten.

BASKAR

sei.. chi.. ithuka kathuna oru nimishathula bayanthiten poi moodhala off panra atha, rendum en ellavu edukkuthu sei.

MURUGAN

boss naan mukiama eludhitu iruken neenga poi off panunga.

BASKAR

dei..

MURUGAN
naan naa..
BASKAR
pooranatha nipatu poi tholayiren.
MURUGAN
(smilling)
BASKAR
ithuku naane paravala

baskar get up from the bench and walk towards the table where the radio has been placed.

baskar takes the radio in his hands, instead of offing the radio he tuned on correctly on the radio. there the radio jockey is speaking about a solar eclipse that happens only once in 1008 years.

radio jockey(r.v)

hi, hello makkale ellarkum vanakum, ithu unga RJ priyan, Shanmuga priyan,naan than pesitu iruken. inikku ennada topic pesarathu nu yosichitu irunthen. apadi oru matter pathi than oru seithi vanthirku. iniku enna na oru suriya karaganam pola,athukana safety measure um eduthukonga. naan ena safety measures solla porathu illa athuku pathula intha solar eclipse vanthu oru special eclipse soldranga. intha eclipse vanthu verum rendu(2) mannerum mattom than irukom ah. ana ithu kitta thatta 1008 varshathukku oru vaati than intha surya graganam sathanama than vanthtu pogathu. intha eclipse oru form of energy release pannum ma. intha energy correct ah equator um greenmeridian link pandra point la meet pannum ma. antha point vanthu external centre of the globe apadinu scientists soldranga. intha point la irunthu oru pattern vazhi whole over the globe ke ithu spread pannum. intha energy namakku nala vazhi kattra postive vibes spread panra energy. intha energy appo kumari kandam solli pandhya manargal ku kedaichathu ippo athey kumari kadam kadal kula moolgi anathala ippo indian ocean la irunthu oru snail maari pattern la south madurai varikum athu touch pannuthu. eppadi namalodya household circuts work pannutho athey maari intha south madurai varikum antha energy store panni konjam konjam ah athu vanthu release agum mah. lit ah kolpathula ithelam evenda kandu pudichathu, kandupudichiven mattum matuna, irukura kolaverila avena konduriven solli irukarvangaluku ungala kana paadal than vanthittu iruku, ungalakana paadal why this kolaveri itho...

After hearing this baskar immediately understand about the time loop happens for him.

MURUGAN

boss ivlo neram vettiya kettadhe ethachu paatu poduvan than atha poi mute pannringa. nalla paatu boss, sound podunga vibe panalam.

BASKAR

ada eruma maatuku poranthavene nee thiruntha matta, hmhmmm. thiruntheve matta da nee.

MURUGAN

naan thirunthi ena india valarasuu aka poren na. naama rendu perum bike thefters. meikirrathu eruma ithula ena peruma. va vanthu utkarubga boss.

BASKAR

rytu uh.. kundi kulla bomb veiklam nenaichen, thapu iven vaila vekanum.

MURUGAN

nolai vayelaye boss.

BASKAR

muruga ah..

MURUGAN

kooputingala boss.

BASKAR

dei gammunu iruda paradhesi paraadhesi.

Soon marvan washed his face and go to the investigation room. baskar looked the frustation and confusion of marvan, so he understands the situation of marvan and him.

when marvan entered the room, varman was ready to play the game and arranged all coins and used his ring as queen.

when they was ready to play, marvan asked the police officer to call the bike thefters.

MARVAN

sir antha rendu perum koopudunga

POLICE

okay sir.

VARMAN

sit and play until they arrive.

meanwhile baskar and murugan

MURUGAN

boss ennaku thani thagam adikuthu, thani enga kedaikum.

boss

en muthrathula kedaikum, saniyene anga iruku jug uh monthu kudi.

MURUGAN(M.V)

ennaya asinga paduthiriya iru.

murugan walks towards the jug and takes the tumbler.

MURUGAN

boss echa thani iruku enga ootha.

boss

en thalaila oothu, engayachu dustbin oothitu kudra.

MURUGAN(M.V)

ennaya porutham varikum nee than dummy dustbin.

murugan walks towards baskar and pours the water over the head of baskar.

BASKAR

nanakettu, enda

murugan

pinnna nee thana sonna thalaila oothuntu paathathuku dustbin la ootha sonna anthan senjen.

baskar wipes off his face.

BASKAR(M.V)

nee than naalu varshathuku nallave iruka matta.

MURUGAN

ippayum soldren nee oru dummy piece.

POLICE

dei rendu perum vaangada. dei unnaku ennada ivlo vethiruku, ithanaikum fan full speed la than da irunthathu.

BASKAR

ethu ithu full speed oducha.

BASKAR(M.V)

ennaya iven koolipatnathu kuda thapa therla itha paathu full speed la pochu nu sonnan pathiya athan ennaku gaanda ah iruku.

BASKAR

ponga varom.

meanwhile marvan and varman

MARVAN

adauthu...

POLICE

sir varanga sir.

MARVAN

avingala antha orathala okara sollu.

VARMAN

good lets start the play.

marvan makes a move and varman makes a move, both were seriously watching the next move of marvan. suddenly baskar and murugan entered to the room.

both of them kneel down on the side middle of the edges.

same focus on the eyes and the coins, suddenly a phone call recieved from a police officer, he declines it.

marvan and varman focused in the game. both of them play very good plays.

marvan defeats a coin from varman.

VARMAN

antha artham illatha, lachiyum illatha vazhkaiku nermaye thedina antha blind person, again it's my turn.

varman move a coin towards marvan.

marvan again defeats a coin from varman.

VARMAN

paravalye evlovo therita. konjam swarasiyum ah poguthala, oru cup tea soldriya ellarkum.

MARVAN

sir ellarkum tea sollunga.

POLICE

ivingalakum ah sir.

MARVAN

ama ya.

the police was suudenly stoped by murugan

MURUGAN

sir ennaku matha tea than pudikathu ennaku chakra gold tea yum apidiye marie gold biscuit mattum koodunga. jewellery kadai karen.

BASKAR

eiy intha enga vanthu enna kekura iru naan deal panren, sir oru moota puffs um rendu cream bun um vangitu vanga.

police looked in a weird manner.

varman splited saliva.

BASKAR

nanakettu...

MURUGAN

loosu alaga marie gold biscuit ah mooki saptrukamla, ennakene varuthu.

BASKAR

muruga naan boss uh da.

MURUGAN

nee oru moota piece uh.

MARVAN

shoooooo...

MURUGAN

en boss naane serupu potruken ennaya pothu shoe nu kathurirarau.

BASKAR

gummanu iruda venali payale.

marvan makes a move and varman defeats a coin.

Again a timeloop occurs for marvan and baskar.
SCENE:7:INT|FOURTH INVESTIGATION BETWEEN VARMAN AND MARVAN.
Marvan was very angry, splashed water and shouted. baskar was listening to marvan's shout and they commenting.

MURUGAN

boss ethachu zip la maatikicha..

baskar

athu zip ila loop la maatikitom.

MURUGAN

loop ah ithu ena puthu kadhai

BASKAR

kadhai ila padam.

MURUGAN

ena padam.

BASKAR

dei gummunu iruda

MURUGAN

boss nee enomo soldra puriyala.

BASKAR

puriincha mattom ena pista aiyurvia. khatija maari.

murugan

athuku edukku gozilla oda moosama kathaanum.

POLICE

sir enna sir achu. kalidhassan ah

MARVAN

kondutanga athane.

POLICE

sir athu mattumila, kondaven

MARVAN

nama station la surrender aiytan athane.

POLICE

ama sir.

MARVAN

anga oru chess board um antha bike thefters um ulla po sollunga.

POLICE

ena iveru thedirendru ivlo nayanaudhayam vandiruchu. correct ah soldraru.

POLICE

dei neenga rendu perum

BASKAR

ulla ponnum marvan sir solla sonnaru athane.

POLICE

ivanum correct ah soldran. ethachu manguukani illa nellikanni saptu nayanothayam vanthucha.

MURUGAN

boss paravalye boss neenga kalakiringa.

BASKAR

ethuah?

MURUGAN

talent.

BASKAR

eppideye pesuna naan aiyuduven vilent.

MURUGAN

violet ah athu saree ku podra colour achey.

BASKAR

enga velai patha

MURUGAN

jewellery shop uh.

BASKAR

enga iruku?

MURUGAN

pothys uh boss.

BASKAR

dei athu jewellery kadai illa da jawuly kadai da en venali payale.

POLICE

dei rendu perum pongada ulla.

BASKAR

porom sir. vada povom.
baskar and murugan went inside the room.
MURUGAN
may you come in.
BASKAR
dei athu may i da.
MURUGAN
ennaku theriyama eppadi mathunanga.
BASKAR
poi thola ulla.
VARMAN
vanga da ennada intha pakam.
BASKAR
bike theft tu na.
VARMAN
seri rytu naan onnu soldren senja neenga thapikalam seivingala.
MURUGAN
sollunga sona senja pannuvom naanga.
VARMAN
aven vera late agum, aven kitta poi enngaluku bathroom varuthu nu sollunga mathathu naan paathukiren.
marvan opens the door, and comes out of the bathroom.
he hears a sound from radio. he go for off the radio, instead he volume on the radio.
then the same program is went on. he realise the purpose of his timeloop.
next he went to the room, there,
baskar and murugan
engaluku bathroom varuthu enga poga.
MARVAN
ahh en thalaila podu.
MURUGAN
(tries to jump on his head but baskar pushes off.)
boss varuthu boss
BASKAR

dei..

MURUGAN

gummunu iruda athane.

BASKAR(M.V)

ennakave athuvum en bitt eh.

MURUGAN

same to you.

MARVAN

aichiiiiee.. po.

BASKAR AND MURUGAN

ah thanks thanks.. vada polam

MARVAN

naan sonnathu than therupi soldren..

the police catches off both of them.

POLICE

engada poringa?

BASKAR

bathroom ku.

POLICE

dei sir ungala kooputaru da.

MURUGAN

avaru than engala vittaru.

POLICE

seri bathroom ethuku poringa?

BASKAR

athu vanthu neraiya peruku pandhi podanum athanala porom.

sir bathroom ku ethuku poringa kekringa sir.

POLICE

athu eppadi da ata time ku rendu perum bathroom varom.

ungalaku ennada varuthu?

murugan symbolically shows two and baskar symbolically shows one.

POLICE

dei ennada mathi mathi kamikiringa.

BASKAR

sir naan antha side ninu onnuku adipen aven intha side la ukanthu povan. ethellam ketutu, thallunga sir

POLICE

sai en lifetime experience la eppadi oru criminals naan paathathathe illa, ponga da pongada.

BASKAR AND MURUGAN

thaaaaank you sir.

POLICE

enna venum nallum pannikonga ana bathroom clean ah irukumunu da.

BASKAR

atha naanga pathukirom sir.

the police enters into the room.

MARVAN

olunga nee sollu intha game eh geme eh than venam.

VARMAN

unnaku thevaiyana details en kitta than iruku, summa kaatama seyala kaami.

marvan takes a deep breath and plays chess in a wise manner.

once he plays the chess, he gains some clues.

VARMAN

antha deaf-blindless allu irukanla, avanuku ipo eppidiachu avanuku kaathu kekum thiran eppadi pochu nu aven therinchika romba arvam kattuna. ipo en turn.

varman again defeats marvan uusing his deja vu activities again marvan and baskar went back to the timeloop.

SCENE:8:INT|fifth INVESTIGATION BETWEEN VARMAN AND MARVAN.

meanwhile baskar and murugan,

BASKAR

ethana thadava da?sopaaaa, mudiyala.

MURUGAN

ivlo mudi vechukitu mudi illa dra.

BASKAR

rasa konjam neram amaithiya irukiriya illanan vaguthalaye koothiriven venali.

marvan again thinks the real problem and he thought tonot to fight with the chess coins, his target was fixed to varman.

when police trying to knock the restroom door, marvan catches the hand of police and,

MARVAN

ena kalidhassan kondaven station la surrender aiytana.

POLICE

ama sir.

MARVAN

poi oru chess board um antha bike thefters um ulla poga sollunga, aven attatha kamichitan ipo en attatha kamikiren.

POLICE

seri sir.

the police officer kept the chess board infront of varman and went off to call the bike thefters.

meanwhile varman was arranging the coins.

later the bike thefters came into it.

the same plan was discussed and tried to execute, suddenly marvanen tered the room. and doesn't allow any one to go out of this room.

baskar and murugan disappointantly looked back and sat down on the bench.again marvan played the chess in a wise manner.

he continously defeated varman coins, varman gives more clues.

marvan recieves a call from a local police officer and every time he declines it.

VARMAN

ipo antha kooruden aven konjam konjam ah avenoda health check panna arammichan. ithanaikum antha kooruden oru ENT SPEACILIST.

VARMAN

antha kooruden ipo edhenala ippadi achu na, avenoda kannuku iruntha optic nerve disturb aiyee brain la irukara antha auditory nerve connection la disturb aiyurkan.

VARMAN

antha disturbance seri pannanum na avenuku oru operation seyanum mah..

VARMAN

avlo sekarama than avenku opreation panna mudiyathu ah.

VARMAN

avenoda brainla oru chinna tumour irukan. atha remove panna than avenaku enga correct ah disturb aiyuriko atha kandupidika mudiyuma ah.

VARMAN

konjam konjam aven atha remove panran.

VARMAN

kadaisiya avenuku antha distubance kandu pidichana ila kandu pidikilaya?

varman uses his deja vu and his prediction power to play his moves.

marvan losed coins and went back through time and finally he keeps a checkmate. he learns every single move in chess.

MARVAN

yes check mate check mate.

VARMAN

mmm.. a good play but not a smart play. oru rajiyatha alikanum na avenuku check mate pota mattom antha rajiyathai jeykala, raja ve kola panna mattom than parika mudiyum.

varman defeats the king of marvan.

again he repeated to his loop.

SCENE:9:INT|sixteenth INVESTIGATION BETWEEN VARMAN AND MARVAN.

marvan was so angry he was waiting for the last clue.

but he was again looped, he shouted and screamed allover in the batroom.

POLICE

sir ena sir achu?

MARVAN

ahann.. nona achu.

POLICE

sir

MARVAN

poi antha chess board poi anga vei.

POLICE

enga sir.

MARVAN

athan ya varman irukara edathula

POLICE

varman ah.. yaaru sir athu.

MARVAN

ahann.. unga appen, kalidhassan kondaven surrender anala

POLICE

ama sir

MARVAN

aven than. po poi soldrathu sei.

POLICE

seri sir.

MARVAN

antha bike thefters um po sollu ulla.

POLICE

mm ok sir

meanwhile,

BASKAR

pathinaru.

MURUGAN

ena naru?

BASKAR

ahan bathroom naru.

MURUGAN

athu ethuku unnaku thefting vitu vera polapu theda poriya.

BASKAR(M.V)

un kooda irukaruthuku bathroom kuda kaluviruven.

MURUGAN

ena pakura.

BASKAR

dei en face cut paarthale theriya venam ma, naan than oru..

MURUGAN

paithiya karen na.

baskar look at murugan with terrible weird look.

MURUGAN

pina ena ennaye vitu poga pakira? un kooda than naan vela papen.

BASKAR

enga bathroom laya.

MURUGAN

chiiii.... avlo kevalama nenaichitiya ennaya.

BASKAR

athuku keelayum nenaichiten.

POLICE

dai rendu perum ulla pangada.

the police went and kept the chess board on the table in the investigation room.

marvan come out from the bathroom, and furiously go inside the room.

MARVAN

inga paaru nee ena panra than ennaku theriyathu, olunga sollu ellam clues um.

VARMAN

naan solanum ah.

MARVAN

mmmm..

VARMAN

chess vilayadu solren.

again marvan and varman playing the chess game.

VARMAN

ena oru maari tension la iruka.

MARVAN

tension la illama pinna edula irupanga. onnume puriya maatingathu ena nadakuthunu ne theriya matingathu.

VARMAN(smile)

hmm..

MARVAN

ennaya sirikara. nee soldra clues ellam enala seriya ve decod um panna mudiyala.

VARMAN

naan oru criminal lawyer. criminal lawyer na criminal cases ah vathadrven illa, ovoru case um criminal ah vathadrven than criminal lawyer.

MARVAN

etho nee soldra, keka nalla than iruku.

marvan defeats coins from varman.

VARMAN

antha kooruden nuku oru ponnu iruku.avala thediren kidnap pannitanga.

meanwhile baskar and murugan.

MURUGAN

boss kolandhiye thoongarathuku ethuku boss kolanthaye kadathanum?

BASKAR

kolandhiye thoonga kadathirangala.

MURUGAN

ama boss kid na kolandha nap na thookum.

BASKAR

unnaya than koopathotila irunthu vazhthaingala.

MURUGAN

ama boss, enga amma ennaya koopathotila irundhu ennaya vazhthanga boss. athanala than naan kasta pattu naalu varsham mechanical enginnering padichen.

BASKAR

naalu varsham ponen sollu padichen solladha.

MURUGAN

bossssss...

MARVAN
hey gummunu irunga da.
MURUGAN
ellam iven than sir.
clues of varman:
VARMAN
aven operation mudinchathum, aven avenoda ponna theda arampichan, theriyavanuku ellam visarichan.
VARMAN
kedasiya aven kedaicha clues vechukitu aven oruthana chi chi moonu pera sandhegum paduthina. onnu antha kidnapping case la involve ana antha police uh, innonu antha sambavam victim ah, innoruthen oru criminal.

varman wants to make a crucial move against marvan. everyone was looking the coin the background music is raising and suudenly stops by murugan.

MURUGAN
sir engaluku sudden ah chu cha varuthu sir.
MARVAN
ai cheee ponga.

varman not defeats the coin of marvan. marvan takes a deep breath.

MARVAN
epo ithu en move.

marvan was curiously waiting for defeating the queen of varman. bgm raises. suddenly a phone call recieves to marvan.

VARMAN
eduthu pesitu va.
MARVAN
excuse me.

SCENE 10:INT|in search of varman|(10:30 AM):

marvan went out side the room and attends the call. it is about a girl was found dead body in factory, he is informing to investigate current situation.

MARVAN

yo ennaya call pannite iruka onnuku ena thaya venum.
local police
sir naan ipo than sir phone panni neenga edukiringa. pathinaru thadava phone ungaluku reach eh aga mattingathu. sir.
MARVAN
seri ena vishayum sollu.
local police
sir inga oru palaya factory la oru ponnu oda dead body iruku sir. neenga vanthu investigate pannanum sir.
MARVAN
yo inga irukara case laye thitu thadumaruren, kalaila oruthen naan kalidhassan konden solli oruthen thali orukaran. mudinchodene naan paakiren. ipo vei phone ah.
LOCAL POLICE
sir sir sir.
when marvan enters to the police investigation room. there varman was missing. not only varman was missing, the bike thefters also missing.
there the police officer is entering into the office.
MARVAN
sir enga sir antha moonu perum.
POLICE
sir ipo than sir naan poi tea vanga ponnen.
MARVAN
yo tea vanga poren nu asalt ah soldra.
MARVAN
avingala kannom ya.
POLICE
irunga sir naan poi thedi paakiren.
the police go to search for them.
suddenly marvan recieves a call from varman from differnt number.
MARVAN
varman.
BASKAR AND MURUGAN

illa un nanban.
MARVAN
dei engada poi tholanchinga.
VARMAN
avingala naan than kooputu vanthen. enkooda than irukanga.
MARVAN
eiyee nee panrathu romba thappu. nee ipo enga iruka.
VARMAN
avinga rendu perum naan kola panna poren.
MARVAN
eiyy eiyy athellam panniradha.
VARMAN
un koodimi ipo en kaiyla. vanthu vangiko va.
immediately varman was anxious to search varman.
he went into the room, and searched for any clues.
there he saw the ring of varman.
immediately he showed to the police.
POLICE
sir enna ring sir ithu.
marvan
intha ring than aven queen coin ku bathila vechu velyadina. poi intha ring oda jewellery details ithu yaaru vangunanga poi kelunga quick.
POLICE
ok sir.
MARVAN
varman thedanum na aven koodutha clues antha kadhaiye vechu than build up pannanum.
MARVAN
oruthananoda kannu kanam na avanuku kannu therla na kooda paravala ana vazhkaye sandikira nimisham therla na aven vazhra vazhkai latchiyum illatha vazhkai.
MARVAN
athey kannu theriyathaven, avenoda kekum sakthi elanthana avenoda lachiyum illatha vazhkai irundupoi arthame illama

poyirum.

MARVAN

antha artham illatha, lachiyum illatha vazhkaiku nermaye thedina antha blind person.

MARVAN

antha deaf-blindless allu irukanla, avanuku ipo eppidiachu avanuku kaathu kekum thiran eppadi pochu nu aven therinchika romba arvam kattuna.

MARVAN

ipo antha kooruden aven konjam konjam ah avenoda health check panna arammichan. vera ena viten

MARVAN

ithanaikum antha kooruden oru ENT SPEACILIST.

MARVAN

antha kooruden ipo edhenala ippadi achu na, avenoda kannuku iruntha optic nerve disturb aiyee brain la irukara antha auditory nerve connection la disturb aiyurkan.

MARVAN

antha disturbance seri pannanum na avenuku oru operation seyanum mah. avlo sekarama than avenku opreation panna mudiyathu ah.

MARVAN

avenoda brainla oru chinna tumour irukan. atha remove panna than avenaku enga correct ah disturb aiyuriko atha kandupidika mudiyuma ah.

MARVAN

konjam konjam aven atha remove panran. kadaisiya avenuku antha distubance kandu pidichana ila kandu pidikilaya?

MARVAN

antha kooruden nuku oru ponnu iruku.avala thediren kidnap pannitanga.

MARVAN

aven operation mudinchathum, aven aavenoda ponna theda arampichan.

MARVAN

theriyavanuku ellam visarichan, kedasiya aven kedaicha clues vechukitu aven oruthana chi chi moonu pera sandhegum paduthina.

MARVAN

onnu antha kidnapping case la involve ana antha police uh, innonu antha sambavam victim ah, innoruthen oru criminal.

marvan

idhellurundhu aven ena soldrana, oru kannutheriyathuven avenoda hearing eluthutan, aven oru ent speacialist. avenuku brain la oru disturbance la ippadi aiyurchu, atha seri panna operation panalam irukum rapo than avenku brain la tumour iruku, athey ella sei panni patha avenoda ponna kidnap pannitanga, pannavunga yaarunu theriyama visarichu avenuku sandhegam vandha oru criminal, oru police, oru victim.

MARVAN

edellam connect panni paartha, antha kooruden avena describe pannirikan. avenuku amma vumilla appa vum elladha nalla hearing use pannirikan. avenoda kolandha padhila yaara solliripan.

police enters.

POLICE

intha ring pathi motha detail um collect panniten, intha ring vangunathu vera yaarum illa varma oda fiance PRIYA, iva than vangirukan sollirukanga kada karenoda owner. avunga than intha ring vaangi engagement ring ah present pannirukangalam. intha priya than sir oru accident case la erandhanga sir oru rendu varshathuku moonadi. antha case koda neenga than moodichinga.

MARVAN

apo antha kulantha than priya va.

POLICE

yaaru kolandha.

MARVAN

onnum illa neenga ponga naan pathukiren.

POLICE

seringa sir.

MARVAN

apana priya va sethathunala, aven moonu pera suspect panna onnu police ah, innonu oru victim ah, innonu oru criminal ah. varma soldrathu paatha victim dhan kalidhassan agavum, naan than antha police officer agvum apo yaaru antha criminal uh???????

AFTER 2 HOURS 20 MINUTES.

SCENE 11:EXT|IN SEARCH OF CRIMINAL|(1:50 AM):

INTER CUT TO:

marvan was eagerly waiting for the answer for the story clue. who is the criminal?

suddenly varman calls marvan

MARVAN

eiyyy, eiyyy varma varma ipo nee enga iruka? yaaru antha criminal sollu?

VARMAN

paravalye ivlo sekerma ah decode pannita. seri naan enga irukenu than venum. konjam nerathuku munadi oru local police officer oru factory sonala anga than nan iruken. kittave oru gun iruku. pakathula antha bike thefters um irukanga.

MARVAN

eiyyeiyyy avingala onnum panatha.

VARMAN

avingala onnum panala ana oruthen eh naan vanthu kolaporen.

MARVAN

yaaru antha criminal.

VARMAN

avanum intha factory ku vandhirukan.

MARVAN

yaaru?

VARMAN

oru detective aven.

MARVAN

peru?

VARMAN

VIGHORAN, ABI VIGHORAN.

MARVAN

hey aven oru detective aven ethuku ippadi seyanum.
VARMAN
nee vanthu aven kitta kettuko. bye.

varman declines a the phone call, and go inside the factory
scene 12:ext|climax|(2:00 PM):
marvan immediatetly come out from the police station.
there the dead body was marked with chalk piece.
vighoran and his assistant veera are discussing the report of the death of the girl was early spoke before scene by marvan and the local police.
veera
sir inga than sir antha ponna oda dead boy irunthu chu.
vighoran
mmm.. nama oru detectives itha eppadi pakanum solli namaku nallave theriyanum.
veera is getting a call from unknown no.
veera
sir etho theriyatha no. irunthu call varuthu.
vighoran
namaku puthusa oru cilent ah iruka pothu poi pesitu vanga.
veera
poi pesitu varen sir.
vighoran
mm.. sekaram.
veera
ok sir.
veera went out from the occasion.
the call was cut, he tried again and again but he doesn't recieve any response.
he entered to the factory. there vighoran was not there. he searched for vighoran and screamed for vighoran.
there a unexpected thing happened. slowly veera took his gun. but two bullet was aimed and shooted by baskar and murugan.
MURUGAN

ena nee mattum than soodivia naanum soodaven, koodu.

BASKAR

etho beach la irukara ballonsoodra maari solra.

MURUGAN

nee koodu enga.

murugan grabs the gun from varman.

MURUGAN

aiyooo... ena pa ivlo weight ah iruku.

BASKAR

pina kaathadi maari parakom ma inga koodu.

baskar again takes the gun. and shoots another bullet.

MURUGAN

boss neenga ivlo neram dummy piece nu nenaichen ana neenga oru super piece uh.

BASKAR

enda naan ena leg piece achi.. gummunu iru.

VARMAN

dei pothum da. gun ah inga koodu.

veera

yaaru neenga?

VARMAN

un varman.

varman points on head and shoots the bullet.

after some times he investigates a vighoran why did he kill priya.

varman

vighorah... unnaku erkanve theriyum naan yaarunu, ennaku thevaiyanuthu ellam oru bathil than ethuku nee priya va konda, sollu neriya time. your time starts know.

vighoran

yaaru priya.

MURUGAN

intha kekara pathuluku olunga pathil sollu veetla jettila aiyy(poop) poniya illaya naanga kekala.

BASKAR

solra.

VARMAN

mm.. avane solluvan.

vighoran

priya va kolla panna sonathu oru terrorist, aven peru kooda enaku theriyathu, aven kolla sonathey money napping kaga than.

VARMAN

money napping ah.

MURUGAN

money napping ah.

BASKAR

kasa thonga vekrathu illada.

VARMAN

apadi na.

VIGHORAN

money napping na eppadi kasukaga kolandhaya thiruduvangalo athey kasukaga kasey thirudrathu than money napping.

VARMAN

kasuga kasa ah. it looks like eye for an eye.

VIGHORAN

ama antha currency la la unique code irukom itha vechu than currency ya identify pannuvanga. antha currency no. la irukara numbers suppose ethavuthu oru palindrome oh illa special no. oh iruntha nadakum. athu neraiya bussiness man ou collection vechirupanga. ana athey maari athula oru dark side iruku. athu sillathu indian oda privacy security base panna no. ah irukom. atha hack panna motha indian privacy seurity crack agum. ithukaga than oru terrorist ennaya hire panni yaaru intha maari currency vechirukanga solli ennaya check panropa than priya peru adi paatuchu. ennaya avala follow pana sonna. ava antha currency ya ipidiachu vanganum nenaichan. ana ava antha currency ya oru oldage home ku charity ya kuduthitan. avala fixed ah vechiruntha, ana ipadi achu nu solli aven nenaichu kuda paakala. athanala ennaya kolla sonnan. naan konduten avala.

VARMAN

wow ippadi oru cheap ana reason nuku en life konduta. seri antha terrorist ena ana.

VIGHORAN

avenoda boss ku therinchathula avenai kondutanga.

VARMAN

avala nee konduta, avenoda boss antha terrorist kondutan, naan ipo unnaya kolla poren.

varman shoots vighoran.

VARMAN

neenga rendu perum poiringa, takunu poiringa.

MURUGAN

enapa posukuanu soototu, thidrenu poga sonna enga poga.

BASKAR

dei va poiravum.

baskar and murugan went outside.

varman sits in a small iron desk(shape).

varman is waiting for marvan

marvan also entered and hit on his fate of his head.

MARVAN

en ippadi panna?

VARMAN

mmm... ohh nee vanthitiya. naan sonna antha kooruden kathai naan mudikala la.

MARVAN

ithuku nee ivingala konda?

VARMAN

ivinga than en priya va kondanga.

MARVAN

athuku nee wait panni court la eevidence mulliyama prove panni nee justice vanganum. nee than criminal lawyer achey.

VARMAN

erkanave naan than sethuten ethuku nee vera, iru antha kooruden kathaiye moodikiren.

varman stands and walk around marvan.

varman tells the remainig story.

VARMAN

antha kooruden oda ponnu partha antha victim oruthen sethutan. yaaro kolapannitanga pola, athu yaaru na antha police officer uh, en kondanga na aven victim eh illayehn. kasukaga victim ah nadichana, athula thapu illa ana antha kolanthaye kidnap than solli aven report summit pannitan. aven antha report ah mathula. athanala ellam naalum antha kooruden sethukiteh irunthan.

MARVAN

therinchirucha.

VARMAN

ellame therinchiruchu. nee than dr.kalidhassan ah konna, athuku antha bike thefters ah almaatum panniruka. antha kalidhassan thapana oru report kuduthathunala nee aven konna. ennaya pathi theriyahuku munnadi ennaya payangarma ennaya visarichika.

MARVAN

(laughing)

ha ha ha... uohhh apa ellam partha maari soldra, ama naan than kalidhassan eh konden, nee court side active irupen partha nee full ah inactive irunthiruka. athanala than konnen.

VARMAN

ethuku nee kalidhassan konna.

MARVAN

engala maar police officer ku vara rendu case um petti case than. engala maari police ku than ena society engala mathikithu. helmet poda sonna mattom ena potringala, ila drink panni drive pannathinga sonna kekiringala ila. engaluku ana mathipu enga society theduthu. intha maari cases than adi ku oru vaati avaniku oruvaati varum, vantha case uh konjam delay achu na athu onnu cbi ku illa intha maari detective ku poiruthu, ila na unnaya maari criminal lawyer ku poirithu, evlo pressure theriyuma. handle panni than case eh takkunu mudikara maari iruku. vera vali ila engaluku.

VARMAN

(deep breath)

vera vaali iruku iru shoe lace mattum katikiren.

varman ties his shoe lace.

varman slightly turns back and takes his gun.

VARMAN

theva illatha vishayuthuku ippayum menakeda kudathu, athey maari than nee. naan ivinga rendu perum kondathu therinchichu athanala...

he points the gun towards marvan, and marvan targets varman with a gun.

MARVAN

naan kalidhassan konnadh therinchichu athanala...

VARMAN

a nice play but not a smart play.

MARVAN

it all ends with the time

VARMAN

yes it ends with time and FATE..

a bullet shot is heard.

THE END

9 798887 331157

Printed by Libri Plureos GmbH in Hamburg, Germany